The New Adventures of
MARY-KATE & ASHLEY™

The Case Of The
Green Ghost™

Look for more great books in

series:

The Case Of The Great Elephant Escape™
The Case Of The Summer Camp Caper™
The Case Of The Surfing Secret™

and coming soon
The Case Of The Big Scare Mountain Mystery™

The Case Of The
Green Ghost™

by Carol Ellis

📖HarperEntertainment
A Division of HarperCollinsPublishers

A PARACHUTE PRESS BOOK

PARACHUTE PRESS

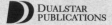 **DUALSTAR PUBLICATIONS**

Parachute Publishing, L.L.C.
156 Fifth Avenue
Suite 325
New York, NY 10010

Dualstar Publications
c/o Thorne and Company
1801 Century Park East
Los Angeles, CA 90067

# HarperEntertainment

A Division of HarperCollins*Publishers*
10 East 53rd Street, New York, NY 10022–5299

1

A GHOST IN THE ATTIC?

"Thump, thump, thump," Patty O'Leary whispered in a spooky voice. "The footsteps crept slowly up the stairs."

My heart started pounding. I held my breath.

My twin sister, Ashley, and I were up in the attic of our California house with a bunch of friends. Clue, our brown-and-white basset hound, lay at my feet.

Ashley and I are detectives. We run the

Olsen and Olsen Mystery Agency—the attic is our office. But we weren't solving a mystery right then. It was the day before Halloween, and we were telling ghost stories.

"Thump, thump, thump!" Patty's voice grew louder. "The footsteps came closer... and closer...and closer!"

My heart pounded harder. I shivered.

Ashley nudged my arm. "It's only a story, Mary-Kate. You know, no one has ever proved that ghosts really exist."

That's Ashley—totally logical. She and I look alike, with strawberry blond hair and blue eyes. But we're really very different. Ashley always thinks things through. I like to follow my feelings.

Right then I was feeling *scared*!

I didn't want to admit it, though. "I *know* it's just a story," I said. "But a ghost story is no fun if you don't let yourself get scared."

"Mary-Kate's right," Samantha Samuels said.

"Yeah," Zach Jones agreed.

Jeremy Burns nodded. "Keep going, Patty."

"I can't just start again in the middle," Patty complained. "I hate being interrupted. You ruined the story, Ashley."

Ashley and I looked at each other and rolled our eyes. Patty is so spoiled, we sometimes call her "Princess Patty."

"Oh, come on, Patty. You can do it," Tim Park told Patty.

Patty stared at the ceiling a second. Then she cleared her throat. "Whoo… whoo! Eerie wails echoed down the hall of the old Bennett house."

I tried not to shiver. Maybe Ashley is right and there aren't any ghosts. But the Bennett house is real—and really spooky. It's a huge, deserted house three blocks from where Ashley and I live. Sometimes you can hear a weird wailing sound coming from it. Just like in Patty's story.

Ashley says it's only the wind in the chimney. I'm not so sure.

"Ellen Bennett sat straight up in bed," Patty continued. "She called out for her parents. But there was no answer!"

"She went downstairs to look for her mom and dad. She checked the living room, the dining hall, the library...no parents."

"Suddenly she heard the footsteps again. Right behind her," Patty whispered. "She spun around and saw...nothing! But the footsteps kept coming closer...and closer!"

I twisted my fingers together. Patty might be a pain, but she sure was good at telling ghost stories.

"Ellen screamed," Patty continued. "She ran back up to her room and slammed the door. Then she heard footsteps on the stairs—closer...and closer. And then...a knock came at her bedroom door!"

Bam, Bam, BAM! A knock came at the *attic* door!

Samantha screamed. Tim yelped. I jumped out of my chair.

Clue leaped to her feet and barked.

Ashley giggled. "That must be the ghost," she teased. "I'll get it."

My heart pounded like crazy as Ashley walked to the door. She pulled it open.

We all stared—and saw...

"Russell Finney!" Patty yelled at our six-year-old neighbor. "You sneak! Why did you try to scare us like that?"

"I didn't!" Russell protested as Clue sniffed his sneakers.

"Well, what do you want?" Patty demanded.

Russell looked at Ashley and me. "I need your help, Mary-Kate and Ashley. I have a mystery for you to solve!"

2

POPSICLE PROBLEM

"**A**re you kidding?" Patty exclaimed. "Russell, you're only six. What kind of mystery could *you* have?"

"An important one!" Russell said.

"You don't have to be old to need a detective," I told Patty. "Go ahead, Russell. Tell us what's going on."

"Wait," Ashley said. "Let me get my notebook." She opened one of her desk drawers and pulled out her detective notebook.

Ashley likes to write things down when

we're working on a case. I usually use a mini tape recorder instead.

Ashley found a pencil and flipped the notebook open. "Okay, Russell," she said.

Russell looked ready to cry. "Somebody stole my Icy-Fruit Popsicle!" he declared. "It was my last one, too!"

"Wait," Ashley said again. "Start from the beginning. When did this happen? And where were you when you noticed the Popsicle was gone?"

"It was this afternoon right after school. I was eating the Popsicle on the front porch," he explained. "Then I went inside to get one of my Kombat Kid toys. When I came back out, the Popsicle was gone!"

"You left an unwrapped Popsicle lying on the front porch?" Patty asked. "Gross!"

Russell looked insulted. "The porch isn't dirty," he told her. "I sweep it every day. That's one of my chores."

Ashley closed her notebook and looked

at me. Sometimes we can read each other's minds. Like now. I could tell exactly what she was thinking—this was no mystery!

"Russell, it's a warm, sunny day," I said. "The Popsicle must have melted."

He shook his head. "It couldn't have—I was only gone for a minute! Besides, the stick was missing, too."

"Well, then a dog probably came by and scarfed the whole thing up," Jeremy said.

"Yeah," Patty agreed. "Who else would want a half-eaten, dirty Popsicle?"

"It wasn't dirty!" Russell insisted. He turned back to Ashley and me. "Aren't you going to solve the mystery?"

There really wasn't a mystery to solve. But I didn't want to hurt Russell's feelings.

"The trail is cold by now, Russell," I told him. "But if it happens again, tell us. We'll definitely investigate then."

"Well, okay." Dragging his feet, Russell left.

"Speaking of Popsicles—what is everybody making for the Icy-Fruit Popsicle contest?" Ashley wanted to know.

The Icy-Fruit Popsicle company was holding a really cool contest. You used Icy-Fruit sticks to make a model of something. Whoever made the best model would win the grand prize—an awesome, sixteen-gear mountain bike.

"That bike is so cool!" Tim exclaimed. "I really, really want it. But I don't know what kind of model to make."

"You better decide fast," Samantha told him. "There's only a week left in the contest. I'm making a model of the Swiss Family Robinson tree house. What are you making, Jeremy?"

Jeremy's face turned red. "I—um, I…"

"Why would Jeremy enter?" Patty interrupted. She laughed. "He doesn't need a mountain bike. He'd just fall off if he tried to ride it!"

"Patty!" I said. Sometimes she isn't very nice.

But the truth is, she was right about Jeremy. He's a major klutz.

"So you're not entering the contest, Jeremy?" Ashley asked.

Jeremy stared at his shoes. "Who wants a dumb mountain bike, anyway?" he mumbled.

"*I* do. My model dinosaur is so big, I'm building it in the garage," Zach said. "I already have hundreds of sticks. But I still don't think I'll have enough to finish. I've *got* to get more sticks!"

"*I'm* making a big carousel," Patty announced. "A purple one—that's my favorite color, so I painted my sticks purple. Everybody knows what a good artist I am, right? It's going to look *sooo* beautiful! I just know I'm going to win."

"Wait a second," I said. "Don't you already have a mountain bike, Patty?"

"Yes, but so what?" Patty replied. "I want another one."

"It isn't fair," Tim muttered. "You should keep out so the rest of us have a better chance."

"I don't know what you're worried about," Patty replied. "You don't have a chance anyway, Tim."

Tim scowled. "I do so. You'll see. I'm going to win!"

"What are you and Mary-Kate making, Ashley?" Samantha asked.

Ashley put her notebook away. "It's in the garage. Come on, we'll show you."

We all went down to the garage. I flipped on the light. Our three-foot-tall sculpture sat on the workbench. A bunch of Popsicle sticks were piled next to it.

"Whoa, the Statue of Liberty!" Zach exclaimed. "Cool!"

Patty sniffed. "Yeah, except she doesn't have any head."

"We're not finished yet," I said.

"It's going to be really good," Samantha told us.

"Yeah." Tim looked worried. "I wish I'd thought of it. Now I'll have to do something even better, like...Mount Rushmore, or the Grand Canyon, or maybe a whole entire city! I want that bike so bad, I'll do *anything*!"

Patty laughed. "You can't make the Grand Canyon out of Popsicle sticks!"

"Who says?" Tim demanded, frowning.

Ashley nudged me in the arm. "Let's get out of here so they won't keep arguing."

"Good idea. Hey, guys," I said. "Why don't we walk around the neighborhood and look at all the Halloween decorations?"

Everybody agreed. We trooped out of the garage.

"Hey, Jeremy, isn't that your brother?" Zach asked. He pointed to three older boys zooming down the sidewalk on their skateboards. One of them waved at Jeremy. "Hey, bro!" he called.

"Hey, Tyler!" Jeremy yelled, grinning. He waved back—and stumbled over a crack in the sidewalk. "Whoa!" he cried, his arms whirling. Finally he caught his balance.

Tyler did a 180-degree alley, then zoomed away. Tim whistled. "Awesome!"

Jeremy nodded. "Tyler is *super* cool," he said proudly. "His birthday is next week. He's going to be thirteen."

"What are you giving him for a present?" I asked.

"It's a secret," Jeremy said. "But it's going to be the coolest present he ever got!"

The sun was starting to set as we walked. All the houses had Halloween decorations in the windows—pumpkins and bats and witches. Lots of the yards held glowing ghosts and skeletons.

Then we came to a house without a single decoration. It was the Bennett house—the one Patty talked about in her ghost story.

The house was totally dark. Some of the windows had boards over them. The chimney was black and crooked. The front steps sagged and there were cobwebs across the door.

"I bet there are bats inside," Tim murmured. "Did you ever see any, Jeremy?"

Jeremy nodded. He lives next door to the Bennett house. "Yeah, all the time."

"What about that spooky wailing noise?" I wanted to know. "Have you ever heard that?"

"And what about the glowing lady's face in the upstairs window?" Patty added. "I saw it once."

"Really?" Samantha gasped.

"It's just an old house," Ashley said. "There's nothing to be scared of."

"Mary-Kate was scared," Patty said with

a laugh. "I saw her shivering when I was telling my ghost story."

"I was not scared!" I insisted. "I was just cold."

Patty smirked. "Oh, sure. It's eighty degrees out!"

Samantha shivered. "Well, all I can say is, *I* wouldn't want to go inside that place, especially at night."

"Oh, come on, you guys," Ashley said. I could tell she was getting annoyed. "The Bennett house is not haunted. For the last time, there's no such thing as ghosts!"

"Okay, if you're so sure, why don't you go in there?" Patty demanded. "Go inside the house—and stay there for a whole half hour. I dare you!"

THE SUPER-SCARY DARE

Go inside the Bennett house? *No way!* I thought.

"Okay!" Ashley declared. "We'll take the dare. We'll go in there and *prove* there aren't any ghosts. Right, Mary-Kate?"

Oh, no. Why did Ashley have to be so brave?

But I had to back her up. I swallowed hard. "Right," I agreed.

"You'll be sorrrry!" Patty said in a singsong voice. "Especially when you lose.

Because whoever loses has to give the winner their Halloween candy. *All* of it!"

"Fine. Except you're the one who's going to be sorry," Ashley told her. "Come on, Mary-Kate."

"No, don't!" Jeremy stepped in front of us. "Patty's right," he said. "The place really *is* haunted. I should know! I hear that wailing noise all the time. And moaning sounds, too. You guys, there's a really *bad* ghost in there. You can't go in!"

Uh-oh. Now I *really* didn't want to go into the house!

"Uh—we better not, Ashley," I said. "It's getting dark."

"You *are* scared!" Patty sneered.

"No, we're not," Ashley said. "But Mary-Kate's right. We don't have time now. We have to be home before dark."

Yes! Saved! I thought.

Then Ashley said, "We'll do it tomorrow."

Nooooo!

"Well…okay, I guess," Patty said. She frowned. "But you have to do it first thing in the morning. It's Saturday—there's no school. We'll meet here at nine o'clock."

"You guys don't know what you're getting into," Jeremy warned Ashley and me. "Messing with a ghost could be dangerous."

"We have to do it," Ashley told him.

He shook his head. "Well, I'm not coming to watch."

"I *can't* come," Zach said. "I have to go shopping with my mom."

"Don't worry," Patty told him. "When Mary-Kate and Ashley run into the ghost, you'll be able to hear them screaming all over town!"

The next morning came much too soon for me. When Ashley and I walked up to the Bennett house, Patty, Samantha, and Tim were waiting for us.

"Are you ready?" Patty asked.

"We can't wait," Ashley told her.

I looked at the house. Even in the bright sunshine, it looked totally creepy. *I can wait*, I thought.

But Ashley was already marching up the sidewalk to the front steps.

I took a deep breath and followed her.

"You won't last ten minutes!" Patty called.

We climbed the stairs to the creaky front porch. "Let's get this over with," I said.

"Don't worry," Ashley told me. "We only have to stay for a half hour. Then Patty will have to admit there's no ghost. Ready?"

I swallowed hard. "Ready," I croaked.

Ashley turned the door handle and pushed.

CREEAAK! Shivers ran up my spine as the door slowly opened. We stepped inside.

CREEAAK! The door swung shut—by itself!

My eyes took a minute to adjust. It was totally dark inside. Dark and cold.

"Do you hear anything?" Ashley whispered.

"No! Why?" I asked. "Do *you* hear something?"

"I thought I heard a noise," she replied. "Kind of a rustling."

Ashley sounded a little nervous. That made me even *more* nervous!

We took out our flashlights and turned them on. I glanced around. We were standing in a huge hall with a wide, curved staircase on one side. Strips of wallpaper curled down to the floor. Thousands of cobwebs hung from the walls.

Suddenly *I* heard the rustling noise. Then I gasped—as a bat swooped down from the ceiling. "Ashley, look out!" I cried.

We both ducked. The bat swept over our heads. It flapped up the stairway to the second floor.

"Whoa!" Ashley gasped.

"Let's get out of here—now!" I said.

"No! We can't quit, Mary-Kate," Ashley argued. "Do you want to lose the bet and give Patty all your Halloween candy?"

"No, but…"

"And it's not just the candy," Ashley said. "She'll call us chickens for the rest of our lives."

I sighed. "Okay," I said. "But if we see any more bats, I'm out of here."

We walked down the hall to a door on the left. We shined our lights inside. A huge dining table sat in the middle of the room. A chandelier dripping with cobwebs hung from the ceiling.

No more bats. And no ghosts. Phew!

The room across from it had no furniture at all. All it had was a big marble fireplace with a cracked mirror over it.

We backed out of the door and walked toward the staircase. Ashley stopped at the bottom of the stairs. She shone her light on the floor. "Look, Mary-Kate."

I glanced down. Drops of green, gooey-looking stuff were spattered near the bottom stair.

"Weird," I said. I started to kneel down to check it out.

"Wait!" Ashley grabbed my arm. "What's that noise?"

I froze, listening.

Thump. Thump. Thump.

A thudding sound was coming from the second floor. Just like the footsteps in Patty's story!

My heart started to pound. We shone our flashlights up the staircase.

Thump. Thump.

A figure suddenly appeared at the top of the stairs. A ghostly figure, green and glowing.

It didn't have a head. Just a shapeless green body.

"A gh—a gho—" I stammered. I couldn't get the words out!

"Uuuuuuuunngggh!" The thing let out a horrible moan.

Then—before I could scream, before I could run...

The ghost swooped down the stairs, straight at Ashley and me!

4

HAUNTED HOUSE HORROR

"**A**aaaahhh!" Ashley and I both screamed.

We spun around and ran for the door. Ashley grabbed the doorknob. Her fingers slipped.

"Hurry!" I shrieked. "Hurry!" I didn't dare look back.

Ashley finally turned the knob and yanked the door open. We burst outside. The door slammed behind us with a loud bang. We flew down the steps.

"What happened?" Samantha cried.

"Did you see a ghost?" Tim demanded.

"We saw *some*thing!" Ashley gasped.

"It was green and shimmery!" I cried. "And it kind of *floated* down the stairs!"

"Whoa!" Tim looked at the house. "So Jeremy's right. There really *is* a ghost in there."

"I told you so!" Patty exclaimed. "You guys lost the dare. You were in there for only nine minutes! You have to give me *all* your Halloween candy tonight. And you better not wimp out on trick-or-treating!"

We walked home sadly. "Patty sure likes saying 'I told you so,'" Ashley said as we went into our house.

"I know," I said. "But we had to run. We couldn't stay in the house with that ghost."

Ashley frowned. "You know what, Mary-Kate? I still don't believe there's any such thing as ghosts."

I stared at her. "What do you mean?" I

asked. "We both saw one right there in the Bennett house!"

"But what if it was fake?" Ashley said. "What if Patty set it all up just to embarrass us and win the dare?"

My eyes widened. I could definitely imagine Patty doing something like that. But still...

"How could she do it, Ashley? I mean, it seemed so real—the way the ghost glowed and everything," I said. "Do you really think Patty could have set that up?"

"There's only one way to find out," Ashley declared.

I groaned. "You mean we have to go back in that house."

"It's the logical thing to do," Ashley said. "We'll take Clue with us. Maybe she'll sniff something out."

"I'm still not sure about this," I said.

"Don't you want to know?" Ashley asked. "Besides, if we can prove Patty set us up, then the deal is off. You can't win a dare by cheating."

I smiled. "That means we'd get to keep our Halloween candy!"

"Right. Now let's go to our office and get to work," Ashley said. "We have a mystery to solve!"

5

THE POPSICLE
PROBLEM RETURNS

Ashley and I hurried up to the attic. Clue followed us, wagging her tail. She can always tell when we're on a case.

The telephone was ringing as we walked through the door. "I'll get it," I said. I picked up the receiver. "Olsen and Olsen Mystery Agency. Mary-Kate speaking."

"This is Samantha!" Samantha cried in a frantic voice. "My Icy-Fruit Popsicle sticks are gone! Somebody stole them!"

"Oh, no!" I said.

"What's wrong?" Ashley asked.

I quickly told her. Ashley picked up the other phone so she could listen.

"Where were the Popsicle sticks?" I asked Samantha.

"On the back porch," she said. "I've been building my model on a table out there. All my sticks were in a bag next to it. When I got home, I wanted to work on the model some more. But the bag wasn't there! All my sticks are *gone*!"

"Are you sure your mom didn't move them?" Ashley asked.

"I asked her," Samantha replied. "She said no. What am I going to do? Now I'll never finish my model in time for the contest!"

"Don't worry," I told her. "Ashley and I will figure out what's going on! We'll be over soon."

When we hung up, Ashley looked at me. "Are you thinking what I'm thinking?"

"Yes. Before we go to Samantha's, let's go check *our* supply of sticks!" I said.

Ashley grabbed her notebook. I picked up my mini tape recorder. We hurried downstairs to the garage. Our model of the Statue of Liberty was still there.

But our pile of extra sticks was gone!

"Russell was right!" I cried. "There *is* a Popsicle stick thief in town."

Ashley nodded. "Now we have *two* mysteries to solve!"

Clue barked.

Ashley pulled out her notebook. "Let's start with motive," she said. "Why would somebody want to steal Popsicle sticks?"

I'm glad we're starting with this mystery instead of the ghost! I thought.

"That's easy," I replied. "The thief probably needs the sticks for the Icy-Fruit contest."

Ashley scribbled it down. "Right. What about suspects?"

"Well, Russell's Popsicle was lying on the porch," I said. "But Samantha's sticks weren't out in the open. And neither were ours. So…"

"So whoever took them knew where they were," Ashley finished.

"Right," I agreed.

We thought about it for a minute. And then the same idea hit us both.

"The only ones who knew where our model was were the people who were here yesterday," Ashley said. She frowned. "You know what this means, don't you?"

I nodded.

"It means the thief has to be one of our friends!"

6

AND THE SUSPECTS ARE...

"**T**his is terrible!" I said. "I can't believe one of our friends would steal those sticks!"

"Me either," Ashley agreed. "I hope we're wrong. But there's only one way to find out. Let's get to work."

We headed over to Samantha's house. Clue came with us.

"Let's see if we can eliminate any suspects," Ashley said as we walked. "Great-grandma Olive says the first thing to do is figure out who *couldn't* have done it."

Our great-grandmother is a detective, too. She taught Ashley and me everything we know about being detectives.

"Jeremy probably isn't a suspect," I declared. "He isn't entering the Icy-Fruit contest, remember? So he wouldn't have a motive to steal the sticks."

"Right. And Samantha is out, too, because her sticks were stolen," Ashley said. "That leaves Zach, Patty, and Tim."

"Hey! Zach told us his model was huge," I said. "He said he had hundreds of sticks. But he was still worried about having enough."

"So he has a motive," Ashley said.

I switched on my mini tape recorder. "First suspect: Zach. Motive: He needs more sticks," I said into the microphone.

Ashley frowned. "What about Patty?"

"She said her model was already finished," I answered.

"Yeah, but remember how she bragged that her purple carousel was going to win?" Ashley reminded me. "Maybe she got nervous when the rest of us told her about our models."

"So if she stole the sticks, nobody else could finish," I said. "And she would have a better chance to win. Hey, yeah! That sounds like something Patty would do! She's got to be the thief."

"Not so fast, Mary-Kate," Ashley said. "We don't have any proof."

I sighed. Ashley is always so logical.

"Besides, we can't leave Tim out," she added.

"Come on, Ashley," I argued. "Tim is our best friend! He would never steal."

Ashley looked worried. "I hope not. But he kept saying he would do *anything* to win that bike."

I bit my lip. Ashley was right, as usual. But solving the mystery wouldn't be any fun if our best friend turned out to be the thief!

When we got to Samantha's house, I clicked on my tape recorder again. "It's ten-thirty A.M. on Halloween. Ashley and I have just arrived at Samantha's house to find out more about her stolen Popsicle sticks."

"Woof!" Samantha's basset hound, Sparky, waddled around the corner of the house. Samantha followed her.

Clue trotted across the yard. The two dogs sniffed each other and wagged their tails. They're good friends.

Samantha led us around to the back porch. "There!" she said, pointing to a round wooden table.

"The model is a partly finished tree house," I said into the tape recorder. "It's really good," I added.

"Thanks. But it doesn't matter now," Samantha said sadly. "It will never be done in time for the contest. It took me *weeks* to collect all those sticks! And now they're gone."

"Did you notice anything else wrong?" Ashley asked Samantha. "Anything missing or out of place?"

Samantha shook her head.

Ashley looked at me. "We have to check out opportunity."

"Right." *Opportunity* is a word we detectives often use. It means when somebody had the chance to do something. "When was the last time you saw the sticks?" I asked Samantha.

"About five o'clock last night," she said. "I worked on the model for a while. Then Mom and Dad and I went out for pizza at six-thirty."

"And you didn't come out here this morning?" Ashley asked.

Samantha shook her head again. "I had breakfast. Then I went back to the Bennett house with the rest of you. I came back here about ten-thirty. That's when I noticed the sticks were gone."

"So the sticks could have been stolen any time between six-thirty P.M. yesterday and ten-thirty A.M. today," I said.

"And you didn't notice *anything*?" Ashley asked. "Think, Samantha. Any little thing could turn out to be a clue."

Samantha frowned. "Well...I saw Tim on the way home from the pizza parlor last night. It was around quarter to eight. He was walking kind of fast down the block. I yelled 'hi,' but he didn't answer."

Oh, no! I sneaked a glance at Ashley.

Tim said he would do anything to win the contest. And Samantha saw him near her house last night!

Tim was looking pretty suspicious.

Was our best friend really the thief?

A Clue from a Cat

"**I** sure hope Tim has a good explanation," Ashley said.

"Me too," I agreed. We were on our way to Tim's house. Clue trotted ahead of us.

"I wish I had a hunch about this case," I said.

Ashley and I work very differently. She makes plans and follows the rules. I forget the rules a lot. But sometimes I get a hunch that helps us solve the mystery.

But so far, I didn't have a single hunch.

And I didn't like where the rules were taking us—straight to Tim's front door!

Ashley rang the bell. Tim's mom opened the door.

"Hi, Mrs. Park," I said. "Could we talk to Tim a minute?"

"You just missed him. He went out looking for more Popsicle sticks." Mrs. Park laughed. "He finally decided what sculpture to build—the Titanic! And now he needs hundreds of sticks!"

My heart sank. We thanked her and went down the steps.

"I guess that doesn't prove anything," Ashley said. "Just because he's looking for sticks doesn't mean he's *stealing* them."

"Right," I agreed. "And he's not our only suspect, remember. There's Zach and Patty, too. Let's go talk to Patty right now."

Ashley glanced down the street. "You know, the Bennett house is only a block away. We might as well check it out."

Oh, no! I was hoping Ashley had forgotten all about our other mystery. "I left my flashlight at home," I told her.

"That's okay," Ashley said. "I brought mine."

I sighed. "I wish you weren't always so prepared."

Ashley laughed. "Come on, Mary-Kate. If we can prove Patty set us up, we'll have even more to talk to her about!"

"Okay, let's do it," I agreed reluctantly. "At least we have Clue with us this time. You'll protect us, won't you, girl?"

Clue wagged her tail. "Woof!"

We hurried to the Bennett house. As soon as we stepped through the creaky front door, I started to shiver.

We stood still for a second, listening. The house was totally quiet.

Clue put her nose to the floor. "Whumpff!" The dust made her sneeze.

She sniffed her way to the stairs.

I peered up the steps as we got closer. The landing was dark and empty.

The drops of green goo were still by the steps—all dried up now. Clue sniffed them for a few seconds. Then she walked past the stairs toward the back of the house.

"Look, Mary-Kate!" Ashley cried, shining her flashlight. "It's more of the green stuff. Clue found a trail!"

I swallowed hard. "A trail to what?" I asked. "The ghost?"

All of a sudden, I heard a slurping sound. My heart started thumping. "What is that?" I whispered.

Ashley shone the light ahead of us. "It's Clue! She's licking up the green drops!"

"Clue, no!" I called. "That might be dangerous! Besides, you should never eat the evidence."

I hurried over and picked Clue up. As I balanced her in my arms, my hand brushed one of her paws.

"Hey. This green stuff is sticky," I said. "And it smells like…"

"Like what?" Ashley asked.

I sniffed my hand. "I can't remember. But I've smelled it before."

Ashley shone her light ahead. "More green drops. Let's see where they go."

We followed the trail along a hall. At the end were three steps down with a door at the bottom. There were more green drops in front of the door.

"I bet this leads to the cellar," Ashley said. She shone her light on the door.

There was a rusty metal clasp above the handle. Hanging from the clasp was a purple combination lock. It was open.

I shifted Clue in my arms and reached for the lock.

CLAAANNNNG!

A loud sound came from behind the cellar door. It sounded like rattling chains.

Ashley jumped a foot in the air and

screamed. I shrieked. Clue barked and struggled to get down.

"Whoooaaa! Leave me alooone!" a low voice moaned from the other side of the door. "Leaaave meeee aloooone!"

"It's the ghost!" I cried. "Let's get out of here!"

We turned to run up the three steps.

"HISSSSSSSSS!"

I gasped—as I saw a black cat at the top of the steps. Its back was arched. Its eyes glowed green.

Ashley grabbed my arm. Her fingers dug in so hard I wanted to scream. But I was so scared I couldn't!

"Leeeaaave meee alooone!" the voice wailed behind us.

"Hisss…Hissss!" the black cat snarled in front of us. It raked the air with its claws.

We were trapped!

8

SCARES AND MORE SCARES!

"**R**rrowwf!" Clue gave a loud bark and leaped out of my arms. She dashed up the steps after the cat.

The cat gave a yowl and raced away. Clue tore after it.

Ashley and I leaped up the stairs. We raced down the hall.

I pointed to a door at the far end. "That looks like the back way out," I panted.

Ashley yanked it open.

"*Aaaahhh!*"

We both screamed—because the door led to a closet.

A closet with a skeleton inside!

The skeleton seemed to reach toward us with its bony fingers. Its hollow eyes stared at us.

"Run!" I shouted.

Ashley slammed the closet door. We tore around a corner—and found ourselves in the big front hall.

"There's the door!" Ashley yelled.

"And there's Clue!" I said. Clue stood at the bottom of the staircase, barking like crazy. I scooped her into my arms.

Ashley pulled open the front door and we raced outside. We didn't stop running until we were halfway down the block.

"That was so scary!" I gasped. I set Clue down.

"I don't know what to think." Ashley's teeth were chattering. "Maybe there *is* a ghost!"

Whoa. If my logical sister thought there might be a ghost—then there *must* be a ghost!

"Let's think about what to do next," Ashley said.

Huh? "What do you mean?" I sputtered. "What more is there to do? The house is haunted. We lost the dare. Case closed!"

But Ashley was shaking her head. "I still think Patty could be playing a trick on us," she said.

"Aaaargh!" I clapped my hand to my forehead. "I thought *you* were supposed to be the logical one! Admit it, Ashley—for once, you're wrong! Ghosts really do exist!"

Ashley looked at her sneakers. "Well, I guess it's possible. *Maybe*," she said at last.

"Anyway, I'm not doing any more detecting right now," I said. "I'm starving! Let's go have lunch."

We went home and ate lunch. Afterward, we stopped by Patty's house to question her about the Popsicle sticks. She lives right next door to us. But nobody was home.

"What next?" I asked.

"Zach's the only one we haven't tried yet," Ashley said. "He's probably back from shopping with his mom. Let's go talk to him and see what we can find out."

When we got to Zach's house, we ran into Jeremy coming out of the gate. He had a paper bag in his hand.

"Hey, you guys. What's up?" he asked.

We told him about the Popsicle stick thief.

"Wow!" Jeremy said. His eyes were wide. "What are you going to do about it?"

"We're here to talk to Zach," I explained. In a lower voice, I added, "He's a suspect. Remember how he said he needed a lot more sticks to finish his model?"

Jeremy looked upset. "But Zach's sticks were stolen, too!" he said. "When he went to work on his model this morning, the sticks were gone. Every last one of them!"

"You're kidding!" Ashley cried.

"I can't believe he didn't call us for help," I said. I felt a little hurt. "I mean, we are detectives."

"Well, anyway, we're here now. Come on, Mary-Kate," Ashley said. "Let's talk to Zach and get all the facts."

"You can't," Jeremy told us. He pointed to a car that was pulling out of the Joneses' garage. "His mom is taking him back to the store—they have to return something. And I have to go home," he added. "I'll see you later."

Jeremy hurried down the sidewalk.

"I guess we're down to two suspects," Ashley said to me. "Patty and Tim."

I nodded. "Let's go find Patty."

As we walked past Zach's house, Ashley suddenly grabbed my arm and pulled me down behind the hedge. "We just found her.

Check out the yard on the side of Zach's house!" she whispered.

I peered over the hedge—and almost gasped out loud.

It was Patty O'Leary! Princess Patty, creeping toward the back of Zach's house!

"What is she doing?" I murmured.

"Maybe she dropped some sticks and came back to get them," Ashley whispered. "Except that wouldn't be very smart."

"Or maybe she dropped something of *hers*!" I said. "Like a bracelet or a ribbon. Something that would prove she was here and stole the sticks."

"Good thinking," Ashley told me. "Let's watch her. Maybe we'll catch her in the act!"

Patty peered into a basement window. She got down on her knees and looked under some bushes. As she stood up, she put her hands on her hips and shook her head.

"She's almost at the back of the house," Ashley whispered. "Come on, we don't want to lose her."

We started to creep around the hedge into the side yard.

Rrring! Rrriinng!

A loud bell made us jump. We looked around. The neighborhood ice cream truck pulled to a stop down at the corner.

I couldn't see the driver. But I *did* see Tim. He was standing at the back of the truck—pulling out dozens of Icy-Fruit Popsicles!

Oh, no! Tim was stealing—right in front of us!

9

PRINCESS PATTY PULLS AHEAD

"**H**urry, Ashley!" I cried. "We have to stop Tim before he gets in trouble!"

"You go," Ashley told me. "I'll stay here and watch Patty."

I spun around and raced down the sidewalk. I couldn't let Tim get caught stealing from the ice cream truck!

When I was halfway there, I started yelling. "Tim! Hey, Tim, stop!"

Tim turned around. When he saw me, he waved. Then he went back to shoveling

Icy-Fruit Popsicles into a paper bag.

"Tim!" I hollered. "Don't do it!"

"Don't do what?" Tim asked as I ran up to him.

"Don't—"

The ice cream man stepped to the back of the truck.

Oh, no. I was too late!

The ice cream man smiled at me. "I hope you don't want an Icy-Fruit," he said. "Because Tim just bought my whole supply."

Bought? Whew! Tim wasn't stealing, after all.

"Here's your change." The man dropped some coins into Tim's hand. Then he climbed back into the truck and drove off.

"Here, Mary-Kate." Tim pulled an Icy-Fruit out of the bag and gave it to me. "Lime-Kiwi. That's your favorite, right?"

"It sure is! Thanks," I said. "But don't you need the stick?"

"It's only one." Tim sighed. "Besides, I'm

not sure if I'll *ever* have enough sticks."

I reminded myself that I still had to question Tim. Even though he didn't steal the Popsicles, he still could have stolen the sticks.

"So, um—what did you do last night?" I asked.

Tim looked a little surprised. "Not much. I worked on my model, mostly."

Hmmm. That didn't tell me much. Then I thought of something.

"Did you watch *Weird Adventures*?" I asked. *Weird Adventures* was Tim's favorite show—and it was on from 7:30 to 8:00. Just around the time Samantha said she saw Tim on her street!

Tim shook his head. "No—my mom needed eggs for a cake. She sent me to my aunt's house to borrow some."

Aha! *Tim's aunt lives on Samantha's block*, I thought. *That must be why she saw him there. He's totally innocent!*

Tim tucked the bag of Icy-Fruits under his arm. "I better go," he said. "I want to work on my model some more. I have to finish it if I'm going to win that bike!"

Tim ran off. I hurried back toward Zach's house.

"What happened?" Ashley asked as I ran up to her. "Where did you get the Icy-Fruit?"

I told her everything that Tim said. "He's innocent," I said. "I'm so relieved!"

"We still need to check out his story," Ashley reminded me. "Good detectives always check the facts."

"I know, I know." Then I asked about Patty. "Did you find out why she was here?"

Ashley shook her head. "She spotted me. So I just came right out and asked her what she was doing. She told me to mind my own business and marched off."

"Hmmm," I said. "I think Patty just became our number one suspect."

I peeled the wrapper off my Icy-Fruit and took a lick. And that's when it hit me.

"Oh, wow!" I cried. "I've got it!"

"Got what?" Ashley asked.

"Remember when I said that the green goo in the Bennett house reminded me of something?" I said. "Well, now I remember what it is. And it's a very important clue!"

THE GHOST IS TOAST

I held up my Popsicle. "The green goo smelled exactly like a lime-kiwi Icy-Fruit!" I declared.

"Are you sure?" Ashley asked.

"Positive," I insisted. "I was just too nervous in the Bennett house to recognize it."

"Whoa. That means there were Icy-Fruits in the haunted house!" Ashley said. "And *that* means..."

"That the green ghost case and the Popsicle case might be connected!" I cried.

"If we solve one, we might solve both."

Ashley folded her arms. "I thought you said the green ghost case was closed," she said. "I thought you said that I was wrong, and the ghost was real."

"Okay, okay, maybe *I'm* the one who was wrong," I admitted. "Maybe—just maybe—there is no ghost after all."

Ashley grinned. "Come on. Let's go back to the Bennett house and look for clues."

"I had a feeling you were going to say that," I said with a sigh.

We headed back to the Bennett house. Even though I knew the ghost was probably a trick, I was still nervous. What if we heard those rattling chains again? And that horrible moan? Or worse—what if the skeleton came after us? Who knew what other surprises were waiting in there?

But everything stayed quiet. We hurried down the hall to the cellar door.

The drops of green goo were still there

on the floor. I dipped my finger in one of the drops and sniffed.

"Were you right?" Ashley asked.

"Yes. It's Popsicle juice for sure," I told her. I glanced at the cellar door. "I guess we'll have to go in there," I said.

Ashley turned the handle, but the door didn't budge. "Hey, now it's locked." She pulled on the purple combination lock. "It wasn't before."

"Somebody locked up after we left," I said.

Ashley kept staring at the lock. "This is weird, Mary-Kate," she said. "The rest of this house is falling apart. But this lock looks shiny and new."

I frowned. "What is a brand-new, purple combination lock doing here?"

We looked at each other. *"Purple!"* we said at the same time.

"It's Patty's favorite color!" I cried. "She must be the one who put it here! You were right, Ashley—Patty set us up so we'd lose the dare. She *must* be the ghost." I glanced down at the Popsicle goo. "And probably the Popsicle stick thief, too. And we've got the proof!" I shook the purple lock.

"Whoa. This lock doesn't *prove* anything," Ashley corrected me. "But it is very suspicious. The first thing we need to do is find out if Patty really put it here."

"Oh, right." My shoulders slumped.

Ashley thought a minute. "Jenkins Hardware Store sells purple combination locks," she said. "Let's go see if they can tell us who bought one recently."

"Right!" I cried. "And it might just be Princess Patty!"

We ran up the stairs and hurried toward Jenkins Hardware. We were on the trail.

And I had a feeling we were closing in— and fast!

11

A BIG SURPRISE

We were almost to the hardware store when we spotted Patty again. She was standing on the sidewalk with a bunch of papers in her hand. We ducked into the doorway of a card shop and watched.

Patty walked up to a telephone pole. She took one of the sheets of paper and stuck it on the pole with a piece of tape. Then she moved on to the next pole.

Ashley and I waited until Patty disappeared around the corner. Then we ran up to the pole and looked at the flier.

LOST, it said in big black letters. MY COUSIN'S CAT. PEBBLES IS THREE YEARS OLD. SHE IS BLACK WITH A WHITE STREAK DOWN HER TUMMY. IF YOU SEE HER, PLEASE CALL PATTY O'LEARY AT 555-7176. REWARD!!!

"I didn't know Patty was taking care of her cousin's cat," Ashley said.

Ashley and I went into the store. "Excuse me," Ashley said to the salesman. "We're looking for a purple combination lock."

"I'm sorry, we're sold out of all our locks," he replied. "I'm still waiting for the next delivery. I sold the last one about…let me see…about a week ago."

A whole week! "Patty must have been planning this trick for awhile," I whispered to Ashley. "She's really rotten!"

"Do you remember who bought the lock?" Ashley asked.

The salesman smiled. "Well, I didn't ask

his name. But he was about your age, with blond hair. And I remember him because he griped about the color. But he said he had to have a lock, so he bought it anyway."

He? Ashley and I stared at each other again. A *boy* bought the purple lock?

"This changes everything!" Ashley declared as we left the store. "Patty didn't buy the lock. She's not a boy! And if whoever bought the lock is the thief, that means Patty's not the thief!"

"Tim isn't the thief, either!" I pointed out. "He's a boy, but his hair is dark brown. Ashley, we just lost both our suspects! Who's left?"

"Zach and Jeremy both have blond hair," Ashley said. "But Jeremy's not even a suspect. He has no reason to steal Popsicle sticks."

"Neither is Zach—his sticks were stolen," I said.

Ashley frowned. "Wait a second. Jeremy

told us Zach's sticks were stolen. But we didn't check it out."

Uh-oh. We broke a major detective rule—always check out the facts for yourself.

We headed back to Zach's house to talk to him. When we got there, his mother said Zach was in the garage. "He has a big surprise to show you!" she told us.

"What do you think the surprise is?" Ashley asked.

"Maybe he finished his model," I said. "The question is—did he finish it with a bunch of stolen sticks?"

When we got to the garage, we stopped in shock.

Zach had a big surprise, all right. But it wasn't his Popsicle stick model.

It was a brand-new, shiny, black mountain bike!

The Last Clue Clicks

"**Z**ach!" Ashley cried. "Where did that bike come from?"

"Do you like it?" Zach asked with a big grin. "It's really cool, isn't it?"

"It…it…," I stammered in surprise.

"It's great," Ashley told him. "But where did you get it?"

"My mom and dad gave it to me last night. They surprised me when I got home from hanging out with you guys," Zach replied. "It's a reward for getting straight

A's on my report card."

"Why didn't you tell anybody?" Ashley demanded.

"I had to go shopping with my mom this morning. And then we had to go back to the store," Zach explained. "I just got home. I haven't even ridden it around the block yet."

Zach patted the handlebars and grinned again. "Look at those tires! Look at that gearshift! And look—it's even got its own water bottle!"

Finally I was able to speak. "It's really cool, Zach. I guess this means you won't be entering the Icy-Fruit contest."

Ashley looked at me. I knew what she was thinking. It also meant Zach wasn't the stick thief. Except for Russell's one stick, the Popsicle sticks were all stolen *after* Zach got his mountain bike. He had no motive!

"Nope. Lucky for me," Zach said. "I

would never have finished my Tyranno-saurus in time." He gestured toward the workbench where his model sat.

I looked at Zach's model. It was almost three feet tall. But most of its head and all of its tail were still missing.

"You really *are* lucky," I said to Zach. "Now it doesn't matter that your sticks were stolen."

"Huh?" Zach looked confused.

"All your extra sticks," Ashley explained. "Jeremy told us they were stolen."

"Jeremy said *that*?" Zach looked even more confused. "I don't get it. Nobody stole my extra sticks. I *gave* them to Jeremy."

Whoa. Now *I* was totally confused, too. "But Jeremy's not even in the contest," I said. "Why would he want your sticks?"

Zach shrugged. "I was too excited about my new bike to ask him." He climbed onto the bike. "I'm going riding. I'll see you guys tonight for trick-or-treating."

Ashley and I said good-bye and left.

"Why would Jeremy lie to us and say Zach's sticks were stolen?" I wondered. "Why would he even want them?"

"There's only one reason—because he's making a model," Ashley said. "He *is* in the Icy-Fruit contest. And *he's* the stick thief."

"But I just don't get it," I declared. "Why would he lie about being in the contest? And does it have anything to do with the haunted house?"

"I don't know. But it's time to find out," Ashley replied. "Let's go, Mary-Kate. Jeremy is about to get an official visit from the Olsen and Olsen Mystery Agency."

We hurried to Jeremy's house and rang the doorbell. His mother opened it.

"Hi, Mrs. Burns," Ashley said. "We came to see Jeremy."

"He went out a few minutes ago," she told us. "I'm not sure where he went. You might try the park—his brother Tyler is skateboarding over there. Jeremy likes to watch."

Ashley and I thanked her. We turned to go. But then I thought of something. "How is Jeremy's model coming?" I asked. "Is it finished yet?"

"Model?"

"You know—for the Icy-Fruit Popsicle contest," I explained.

Mrs. Burns frowned. "Jeremy hasn't said anything about a model. *Or* a contest."

Huh? I shook my head. This case kept getting stranger and stranger!

"She didn't know what we were talking about," I said to Ashley as we walked down the steps. "Weird."

"Very weird," Ashley agreed.

"What should we...hey, look!" I said. I pointed.

On Jeremy's lawn lay an Icy-Fruit Popsicle stick.

I picked the stick up. Then I glanced

across the yard and saw…the old Bennett House.

I looked at the stick again. Then at the house.

And then it hit me.

"I just got an idea, Ashley!" I cried. "Come on—we have a ghost to catch!"

CASES CLOSED!

I explained my hunch on the way to the Bennett house.

"It makes perfect sense, Mary-Kate!" Ashley declared as we went up the front steps. "It explains everything!"

"Right," I agreed. "Now all we have to do is prove it."

"Keep quiet. He might be here," Ashley warned.

"I'm counting on it," I said.

I opened the front door. It creaked faintly.

As we tiptoed inside, Ashley turned on her flashlight.

Two green eyes glowed at us from the curving staircase.

I clapped my hand over my mouth so I wouldn't scream.

"It's okay," Ashley whispered. "It's the cat we saw before."

The black cat crept toward us, keeping low to the ground.

We stood still so we wouldn't spook it.

The cat gave a soft meow. It rubbed against my leg.

I smiled and stroked its head. It started purring. Then it rolled onto its back.

"You're not an attack cat, are you?" I whispered. "You were just scared before."

"Look, Mary-Kate!" Ashley murmured. "It has a white streak on its tummy. I bet it's Pebbles—the cat on Patty's flier! We should take her with us when we leave."

"Good idea." I patted Pebbles one more

time. Then Ashley and I tiptoed down the hall to the basement door.

Ashley shone her light on the door. The lock was open.

We nodded at each other. Then we raced down the three steps and threw open the basement door.

"Jeremy!" I shouted.

"Aaahhh!" Jeremy hollered. He spun around.

"I knew it!" I cried. "I knew you would be here!"

Jeremy opened his mouth to speak. But no words came out.

Ashley and I looked around. In the middle of the room was a big table. On top of it was Jeremy's model—an old-fashioned railroad train.

The model was huge. It had tracks, an engine, boxcars, a coal car, and a caboose. It had crossing signals and a train station. It even had a bridge. It was awesome!

And it was made completely with Popsicle sticks!

"Wh-what…" Jeremy stammered. "What are you doing here?"

"Solving a case," Ashley said. "We knew the Popsicle stick thief had to be one of our friends. At first we thought it was Tim. Then Patty. But then the salesman at Jenkins Hardware said a blond-haired boy bought a purple combination lock, just like the one on that door."

"And we talked to Zach," I said. "His sticks weren't stolen. He told us he gave them away—to you."

"You're the thief, aren't you, Jeremy?" Ashley asked. "You took Samantha's sticks. And ours."

Jeremy's face turned bright red.

"And you're the green ghost, too," I declared. "You wanted to scare us away from this house because this is where you were hiding your model."

Jeremy hung his head. "You're right," he admitted. "You figured it all out."

"I still can't believe it," Ashley said. She folded her arms. "*You're* the green ghost? It seemed so real—I almost started believing in ghosts! How did you do it?"

"I found an old piece of green cloth in one of the upstairs rooms," Jeremy explained. "I put it over my head and held a flashlight under my shirt so it would look like I was glowing."

"And the skeleton?" Ashley asked.

"Oh, that." Jeremy shrugged. "It's a plastic model from one of those kits—you know, the kind you put together. I love those kits. I build models of just about everything."

"There's just one thing I don't get," I said. "Why didn't you just admit you were in the contest in the first place? And why are you building your model *here*?"

"Because I didn't want *anyone* to know,"

Jeremy explained. "I couldn't take a chance that my brother would find out. I want to win that bike for his birthday. Tyler is so cool. I just want to give him something really great."

Jeremy sighed. "But then I ran out of sticks. I knew I wouldn't be able to finish unless I had lots more. That's why I took yours and Samantha's."

"And Russell Finney's, too?" Ashley asked.

Jeremy shook his head. "That must have been a dog, like I said. But that was what gave me the idea. Anyway, after I stole the sticks, I started to feel really terrible. So when Zach told me he was dropping out of the contest, I asked him for his extras—so I could pay you guys back. See?"

Jeremy pointed to two paper bags next to his sculpture. One had Samantha's name written on it. The other had our names.

I opened the one with Ashley's and my

name. Inside were hundreds of sticks. Way more than Jeremy took from us.

"I was going to drop them at your house when you weren't home," Jeremy told us. "And Samantha's, too. That way you could finish your models."

"What about *your* model?" Ashley asked.

"It's finished," Jeremy said. "I'm sorry, you guys. I'm really sorry. I know I was wrong. I just want a chance to win that bike for Tyler. Please don't tell everybody what I did!"

Ashley and I looked at each other. I raised my eyebrows.

Ashley gave me a little nod.

"Okay," I told Jeremy. "We won't tell. But you have to drop Samantha's sticks off at her house right now!"

"I will!" Jeremy said. "Thanks. I owe you—big time!"

"You sure do." I grinned. "And I have a great idea about how you can pay us back."

An hour later Ashley and I and all our friends gathered on the sidewalk in front of the Bennett house.

Ashley and I were in clown costumes. Samantha was dressed as a space alien. Zach was Batman, and Tim was a pirate.

Patty wore a long purple dress and a sparkling crown. She was a princess—of course.

"Okay, where's Pebbles?" Patty asked, looking around. "I don't see her."

Ashley and I grinned at each other. Pebbles was safe at our house. But we hadn't told Patty—yet. All we told her was that we knew where her cat was. And all she had to do was get it.

I couldn't wait!

"Where is she?" Patty repeated.

"She's in there." I pointed to the Bennett house.

Patty stared at the old, rundown house.

Her eyes went wide. She gulped.

"Pebbles is scared of Ashley and me," I said. "So you'll have to come in with us to get her."

Patty licked her lips. "Go inside the B-B-Bennett house?" she stammered.

"Come on, Patty," Ashley teased. "You're not scared of a haunted house, are you?"

Patty gulped again. "N-No."

"Great," I said. "Let's go."

Everybody else waited outside while we went in.

Patty jumped when the door creaked. She gasped when it slammed. She squealed when I touched her arm.

"I bet Pebbles is up there," I said. I shone my flashlight on the stairs.

Patty swallowed hard. Then she walked toward the stairs. Ashley and I followed.

Patty climbed up the first step. Then the second.

Claannk! Claannnk!

Chains rattled from the top of the stairs.

"Leaavve meee alooonnne!" a horrible voice moaned. "Leaaavvve meeeee aloooonnne!"

"Aaaahhh!" Patty shrieked. She leaped off the stairs, yanked open the door, and raced out of the house. "Aaahhhh!"

The door slammed behind her.

Jeremy peered down from the top of the stairs. He was holding a long chain. "Was that okay?" he asked.

"It was perfect!" I told him.

Ashley and I gave each other a high five. We solved two mysteries, found a lost cat, and scared Princess Patty—all in the same day!

Boy, do I love being a detective!

Hi from the both of us,

We were so excited to spend an entire vacation at Big Ski Mountain! We couldn't wait to ski and snowboard and build snowmen!

But then weird things started happening at the Lodge. The kitchen was trashed—and something began leaving giant footprints in the snow! We heard a scary story about a monster who lived on the mountain. Was it true? Or was someone else behind all the accidents?

Want to read more about this monster of a case? Here's a sneak peek at our newest adventure: *The Case of the Big Scare Mountain Mystery.*

See you next time!

Love,

Ashley Olsen + Mary-Kate Olsen

The Case Of The
Big Scare Mountain Mystery

I stared at the ski lodge kitchen. Fruit and vegetables had been tossed out of the big refrigerators. Pots and pans were scattered all over the place. A carton of eggs was smashed on the floor.

Who in the world did this?

A big box sat upside down in the middle of the floor. The label said it held packets of powdered hot chocolate! But now the packets were shredded, and the brown powder was all over the kitchen tiles.

"Look, Ashley." I pointed. A trail of chocolate powder led to the back door. "Whoever did this might have left footprints outside!"

We picked our way to the open back door.

"If there were any footprints, they're gone now," Ashley said. "So is the cocoa trail. It snowed during the night. No clues."

"Why are you bothering to look for clues?" Natasha Benson demanded. "I'm telling you, I know who did this. It was the Big Scare Mountain Monster!"

The lodge manager, Mr. Butterfield, frowned. "Not that silly myth again!" he said. "There is no monster. And it's Big *Ski* Mountain, not Big Scare Mountain."

"I saw the monster myself!" Natasha declared. "It's huge and it has long shaggy hair and it makes horrible grunting sounds. It almost grabbed me once."

Ashley rolled her eyes. We'd heard lots of Natasha's tall stories last night. This sounded like another one!

Natasha frowned at all of us. "There really is a monster," she insisted. "Just wait—you'll see!"

Mr. Butterfield shook his head. "Girls, I need you out of the kitchen," he told us. "The police are on their way. I don't want you underfoot."

Ashley nudged my arm. "I guess we don't need to investigate with the police on the case," she said.

"Right," I agreed. "Let's ski. Come on, Natasha!"

We grabbed our coats and headed for the slopes.

The Big Ski Mountain Lodge sits halfway up the mountainside. Ashley and I skied behind Natasha as she led us down one of the slopes, then across a ridge.

When we reached another slope, Natasha stopped. She pushed her goggles up and squinted in the glare. "This is the best slope. See? There's nobody else around," she said, pointing down.

"Perfect!" I said. "Let's go!"

I dug my poles into the snow. But before

I could push off, Natasha let out a scream.

Ashley and I stared at her. "What's wrong?" Ashley cried.

"Look!" Natasha shouted. She pointed down the slope. "It's the Big Scare Mountain Monster!"

Oh, sure, I thought. I wasn't even going to bother looking.

Then Ashley gasped. So I looked.

I gasped, too. My heart began to pound.

A figure was disappearing into the trees. A figure covered with long, shaggy hair that flapped in the wind!

It scrambled along, all hunched over. It looked like some kind of…monster!

Ashley and I stared at each other with our mouths open.

Could Natasha be right?

Was there really a monster on Big Ski Mountain?

OFFICIAL RULES

1. No purchase necessary.

2. To enter complete the official entry form or hand print your name, address, and phone number along with the words "The New Adventures of Mary-Kate & Ashley™ Malibu Beach Sweepstakes" on a 3 x 5 card and mail to: The New Adventures of Mary-Kate & Ashley™ / Malibu Beach Sweepstakes c/o HarperCollins Publishers Attn: Department AW-Malibu, 10 East 53rd Street, New York, NY 10022. All entries must be postmarked no later than December 31, 1999. Enter as often as you wish, but each entry must be mailed separately. One entry per envelope. Partially completed, illegible or mechanically reproduced entries will not be accepted. Sponsors are not responsible for lost, late, mutilated, illegible, stolen, postage due, incomplete or misdirected entries. All entries become the property of Dualstar Entertainment Group, Inc., and will not be returned.

3. Sweepstakes open to all legal residents of the United States, who are between the ages of five and twelve by December 31, 1999 excluding employees and immediate family members of HarperCollins, Parachute Properties and Parachute Press, Inc., and their respective subsidiaries and affiliates, officers, directors, shareholders, employees, agents, attorneys and other representatives (individually and collectively "Parachute"), Dualstar Entertainment Group, Inc. and its subsidiaries and affiliates, officers, directors, shareholders, employees, agents, attorneys and other representatives (individually and collectively "Dualstar"), and their respective parent companies, affiliates, subsidiaries, advertising, promotion and fulfillment agencies, and the persons with whom each of the above are domiciled. Offer void where prohibited or restricted.

4. Odds of winning depend on total number of entries received. All prizes will be awarded. Winners will be randomly drawn on or about January 14, 2000 by HarperCollins Publishers whose decisions are final. Potential winner will be notified by mail and potential winner will be required to sign and return an affidavit of eligibility and release of liability within 14 days of notification, or another winner will be chosen. Prizes won by minors will be awarded to parent or legal guardian who must sign and return all required legal documents. By acceptance of the prize, winner consents to the use of his/her name, photograph, likeness, and personal information by HarperCollins, Parachute, and Dualstar, for publicity purposes without further compensation except where prohibited.

5. One (1) Grand Prize Winner will win a trip to Malibu Beach and the chance to meet Mary-Kate and Ashley Olsen. The Grand Prize Winner will also receive a surf board autographed by Mary-Kate and Ashley. HarperCollins, Parachute, and Dualstar, reserve the right to substitute another prize of equal or greater value in the event that the winner is unable to receive the prize for any reason. All expenses not stated are at the winner's sole expense. (Total approximate value:$3,200.00). 100 First Prize Winners will receive a copy of *You're Invited to Mary-Kate & Ashley's Hawaiian Beach Party* video (Total approximate value $12.95 each).

5a. HarperCollins Publishers will provide the contest winner and a) [two parents] or b) [a legal guardian and a second child] with round-trip air transportation from major airport nearest winner to Los Angeles, standard hotel accommodations for a two night stay, an autographed surf board, and the chance to meet Mary-Kate and Ashley Olsen, subject to availability. Trip must be taken within one year from the date prize is awarded. All additional expenses including taxes, meals, gratuities, and incidentals are the responsibility of the prize winner. Airline, accommodation and other travel arrangements will be made by HarperCollins in its discretion. HarperCollins reserves the right to substitute a cash payment of equal value for the Grand Prize. Travel and use of accommodation are at risk of winner and HarperCollins does not assume any liability.

6. Only one prize will be awarded per individual, family, or household. Prizes are non-transferable and cannot be sold or redeemed for cash. Any federal, state, or local taxes are the responsibility of the winner.

7. Additional terms: By participating, entrants agree a) to the official rules and decisions of the judges which will be final in all respects; and b) to release, discharge and hold harmless HarperCollins, Parachute, Dualstar, and their affiliates, subsidiaries and advertising and promotion agencies from and against any and all liability or damages associated with acceptance, use or misuse of any prize received in this sweepstakes.

8. To obtain the name of the winner, please send your request and a self-addressed stamped envelope (excluding residents of Vermont and Washington) to The New Adventures of Mary-Kate & Ashley™ Malibu Beach Sweepstakes, c/o HarperEntertainment, 10 East 53rd Street, New York, NY, 10022.

PARTI IN STYLE
WITH MARY-KATE AND ASHLEY!

You'll Go Simply Wild for Their All New Video.

YOU'RE INVITED TO MARY-KATE & ASHLEY'S™ FASHION PARTY™

Each Video includes a Mary-Kate and Ashley Sampler book from HarperEntertainment.

Own it on video this fall.

DUALSTAR
VIDEO

Two Times the Fun!
Two Times the Excitement!
Two Times the Adventure!

Check Out All Eight *You're Invited* Video Titles...

... And All Four Feature-Length Movies!

DUALSTAR VIDEO

And Look for Mary-Kate & Ashley's Adventure Video Series.

KidVision
A DIVISION OF
WARNERVISION
ENTERTAINMENT

**Load up
the one-horse
open sleigh.
Mary-Kate and Ashley's
Christmas Album
is on the way.**

It doesn't matter if you live around the corner...
or around the world....
If you are a fan of Mary-Kate and Ashley Olsen,
you should be a member of

Mary-Kate + Ashley's Fun Club™

Here's what you get
Our Funzine™
An autographed color photo
Two black and white individual photos
A full sized color poster
An official Fun Club™ membership card
A Fun Club™ School folder
Two special Fun Club™ surprises
Fun Club™ Collectible Catalog
Plus a Fun Club™ box to keep everything in.

To join Mary-Kate + Ashley's Fun Club™, fill out the form below
and send it along with

U.S. Residents	$17.00
Canadian Residents	$22.00 (US Funds only)
International Residents	$27.00 (US Funds only)

Mary-Kate + Ashley's Fun Club™
859 Hollywood Way, Suite 275
Burbank, CA 91505

Name:_____

Address:_____

City:_____ St:_____ Zip:_____

Phone: (_____) _____

E-Mail:_____

Check us out on the web at
www.marykateandashley.com